The Zero-G Headache

Books by Robert Elmer

ASTROKIDS

#1 / *The Great Galaxy Goof*
#2 / *The Zero-G Headache*

PROMISE OF ZION

#1 / *Promise Breaker*
#2 / *Peace Rebel*
#3 / *Refugee Treasure*

ADVENTURES DOWN UNDER

#1 / *Escape to Murray River*
#2 / *Captive at Kangaroo Springs*
#3 / *Rescue at Boomerang Bend*
#4 / *Dingo Creek Challenge*
#5 / *Race to Wallaby Bay*
#6 / *Firestorm at Kookaburra Station*
#7 / *Koala Beach Outbreak*
#8 / *Panic at Emu Flat*

THE YOUNG UNDERGROUND

#1 / *A Way Through the Sea*
#2 / *Beyond the River*
#3 / *Into the Flames*
#4 / *Far From the Storm*
#5 / *Chasing the Wind*
#6 / *A Light in the Castle*
#7 / *Follow the Star*
#8 / *Touch the Sky*

01A

ROBERT ELMER

The Zero-G Headache

BETHANY BACKYARD®
www.bethanyhouse.com

The Zero-G Headache
AstroKids

Cover and text illustrations by Paul Turnbaugh
Cover design by Lookout Design Group, Inc.

Published by Bethany House Publishers
A Ministry of Bethany Fellowship International
11400 Hampshire Avenue South
Minneapolis, Minnesota 55438
www.bethanyhouse.com

Printed in the United States of America by
Bethany Press International, Minneapolis, Minnesota 55438

Library of Congress Cataloging-in-Publication Data

Elmer, Robert.
The Zero-G headache / by Robert Elmer.
p. cm. — (AstroKids ; 2)
Summary: When Zero-G, a hot new space-rock boy band, arrives at the space station, the AstroKids learn a valuable lesson about hospitality.
ISBN 0-7642-2357-7 (pbk.)
[1. Space stations—Fiction. 2. Christian life—Fiction. 3. Science fiction.] I. Title.
PZ7.E4794 Ze 2000
[Fic]—dc21

00-009972

To Jeremy,

the musician.

THIS STORY WAS ENGINEERED AND WRITTEN BY...

ROBERT ELMER is an Earth-based author who writes for life-forms all over the solar system. He was born the year after the first *Sputnik* satellite was launched, and grew up while Russia and the United States were racing to put a man on the moon. *Why not a boy on the moon?* he wanted to know. Today, Robert lives with his wife, Ronda, their three kids, and a non-computerized dog friend. Their house is about ninety-three million miles from the sun.

Contents

MEET THE AstroKids

Lamar "Buzz" Bright

Show the way, Buzz! The leader of the AstroKids always has a great plan. He also loves Jupiter ice cream.

Daphne "DeeBee" Ortiz

DeeBee's the brains of the bunch—she can build or fix almost anything. But, suffering satellites, don't tell her she's a "GEEN-ius"!

Theodore "Tag" Ortiz

Yeah, DeeBee's little brother, Tag, always tags along. Count on him to say something silly at just the wrong time. He's in orbit.

Kumiko "Miko" Sato

Everybody likes Miko the stowaway. They just don't know how she got to be a karate master, or how she knows so much about space shuttles.

Vladimir "Mir" Chekhov

So his dad's the station commander and Mir usually gets his way? Give him a break! He's trying. And whatever he did, it was probably just a joke.

1 Space Headache

It should have worked.

Memory circuits okay? Check.

Power supply online? Check-check.

Sensors working? Check-check-check.

It even looked like a real drone. It had a round silver body about the size of a basketball. Two red camera-sensor eyes. And three long arms with grabber-claw hands on the ends.

Only, this one belonged to me, DeeBee Ortiz.

Never mind that it was made out of spare parts. I thought it looked kind of cute, actually. And when I flicked on my remote control, it should have floated about a meter off the floor.

But instead, that's when all the trouble started.

Okay, so a few parts were still missing. Minor memory chips, power phase controls, that sort of thing. I figured I'd add them later. I can usually find extras in my dad's shop. He's the chief solar tech on *CLEO-7*, our space station. Mr. Fix-It.

But, suffering satellites! I didn't expect what was about to happen. Neither did the other AstroKids who walked into the shop just then.

"Hey, big *retsis*!" yelled Tag. "GUESS WHAT!"

Did I say "walked" in? Not quite. Tag, Miko, and Buzz came busting into Dad's workshop as if they were shot out of a loose laser cannon.

I'd expect that from Tag. Because little brothers . . . well, you know what I mean. Like his whole backward-words thing. Saying "retsis" instead of "sister." Get it? Ha-ha. I think it's pretty lame, too, IMHO. (That stands for In My Humble Opinion. It's kind of the way I talk. You'll catch on.)

Now, Buzz, who is definitely *not* a pest, was just a little ways behind Tag. And Miko? I could tell she was excited, but she didn't say much. Of course, she hasn't said much since she stowed away on a shuttle to get here to *CLEO-7*.

QUESTION 01:

So what's all this about *CLEO-7*?

ANSWER 01:

Glad you asked. CLEO stands for Close Earth Orbit. It's a big space station where the Astro-

Kids live (that's me and my friends). It's 400,000 kilometers from Earth and right near the moon. Can you figure out how many miles that is? (There are about eight kilometers for every five miles.) It's pretty easy, actually. But then, everyone says I'm really smart. I'm not, really.

Now, about that poor drone. Just as the other AstroKids came running in, it started spinning—right there on the floor. A warning buzzer went off, too, which must have scared Tag. (It doesn't take much to scare Tag. Say "boo," and he hits the ceiling.)

"Yaa!" Tag slipped and hit the floor, scrunched the drone, and spun on his back. (The floor in the shop is kind of slippery.)

"Watch it!" called Buzz. He tripped over Tag. Miko was too close behind *him* to stop, so she went flying, too.

"Are you all right?" I asked, but the drone didn't answer. My poor little machine just kept spinning as if someone had hit the Fast-Forward button. Over and over. Faster and faster. One of his arms loosened up and slapped Tag in the back.

WHAP!

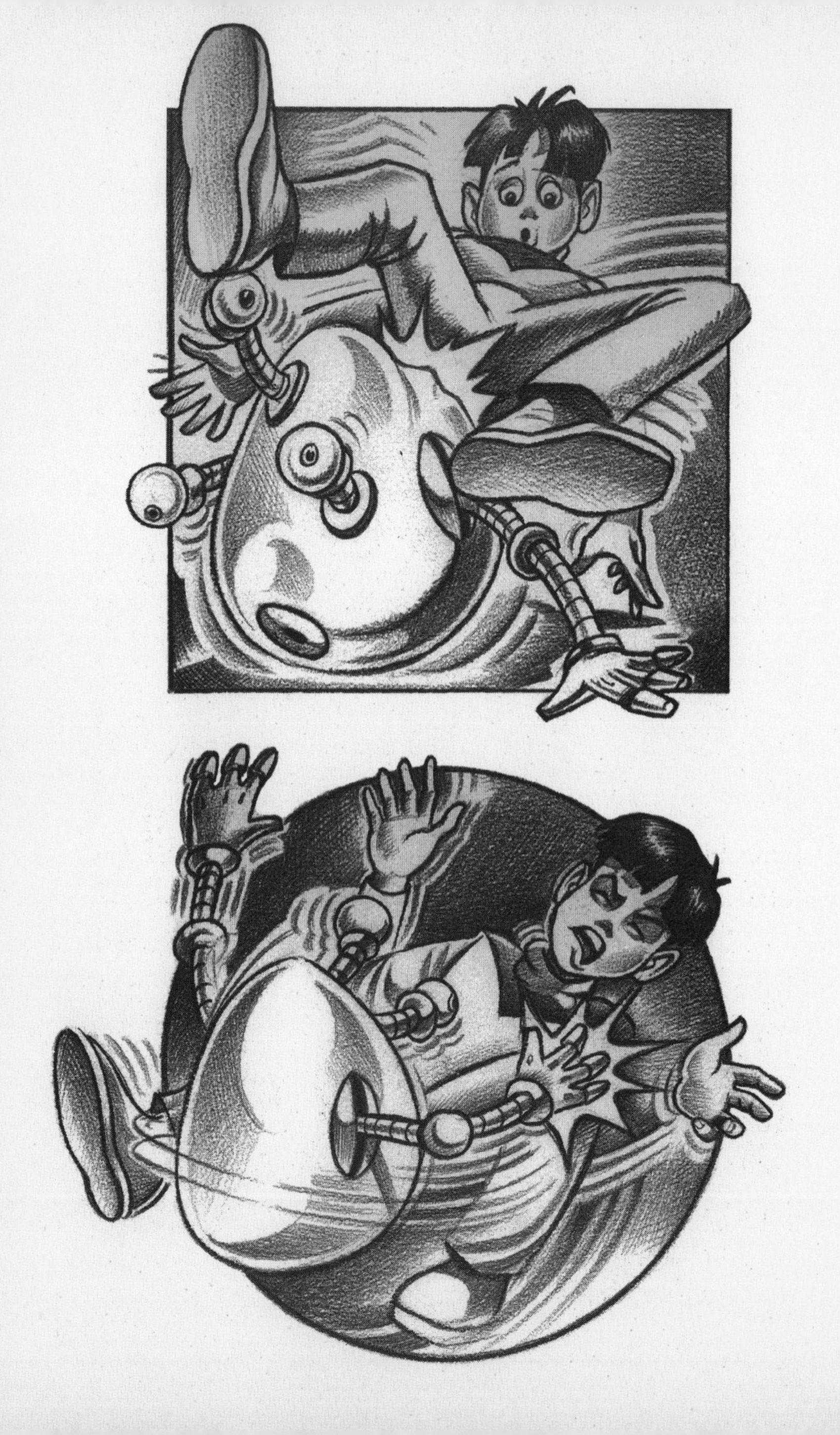

"Ow!" Tag tried to get out of the way.

WHAP, again!

"If this thing would just—"

WHAP, a third time!

"—leave me alone."

By then, the drone was finally slowing down. Maybe it was all the whapping. It made a sort of *whooosh* sound, like it was breathing its last breath. (Drones don't really breathe, though.)

Finally, Buzz reached out and caught it.

"Sorry. I think it's broken." He stood up and held it out to me as Tag got up, too.

I groaned when I saw the poor drone. It was almost working before, and now . . .

"I'm reaalllly sorry, DeeBee." Tag looked up at me with his big brown eyes. I knew he didn't mean to fall on it. I just wished he were more careful sometimes.

"I know. It's all right." I took my drone and turned back to the table. I totally hate it when things don't work.

But it wasn't just that. If I didn't get this drone working in four days, I wasn't going to pass my drone-tech class at school. And I'd been working on that class for a long, long time.

Ahh! Four days!

"We haven't even told you what we came to tell you!" Tag perked back up.

I took a phaser-probe and poked at the mess of light-wires sticking out of the drone's arm. "This is going to take at least another two days to fix," I said.

"Don't you even want to know that Zero-G's Gravity Groove Tour, 2175, is coming this way?"

Zero-G?

2 Way 2 Noisy

"You know, DeeBee. *Zero-G.*"

My little brother looked at me as if I'd just stood under a meteor shower. Like, anybody at the controls?

But I knew. Of course I'd heard of Zero-G before. They were the galaxy's hottest space-rock boy band. They sang . . . kind of. They danced. They had the latest instruments.

QUESTION 02:

What kind of a weird name is Zero-G?

ANSWER 02:

Good question! It stands for *zero gravity*. You know, when the ambient gravitational force is weakened by a factor of—

QUESTION 03:

Hold it! Hold it! Can you explain in English?

ANSWER 03:

Oh, sorry. It just means being weightless. Floating around in space. Good name for a space band, right?

"Three of them are brothers," said Buzz.

So what? I thought. Did that make their music better? I wasn't sure. They were probably nice guys. But IMHO, their songs sounded like a cross between a sun storm and a cracked rocket booster. Personally, I like old jazzy stuff way better.

But you think I'd tell that to anyone on the station? No way!

"They're even making a holo-vid of their tour, DeeBee," Tag told me.

"That's great." I kept working on my project. Or tried to.

"And we could be in it, if only we could get them to stop here on *CLEO-7*."

"Um-hmm."

"I think it would be fun," giggled Miko. "They're all so cute."

And Tag again: "But we need DeeBee's *sniarb* to help us figure how to get them to *CLEO-7*."

Sniarb. Brains, spelled backward.

Maybe they could guess from my voice I wasn't a huge fan. No one said anything for a minute.

"Come on, you guys." Buzz turned back toward the door. "We didn't mean to bother you, DeeBee. You're busy. Maybe we'll come back later."

That's the thing about Buzz. See, everybody likes him, including me. He's the kind of guy people trust when they have to decide something. Like, "Should we do this, Buzz?" He has good ideas.

"No, wait!" I sighed. "Zero-G is my fav . . ." The word stuck in my throat. I couldn't say it. "I mean, I'm sure they're . . . uh . . . great . . . pals."

I didn't want to let them down. Techno-nerds like me need all the friends we can get. And if Miko and Buzz liked Zero-G, well, maybe I could pretend.

But this wasn't going to be easy.

So fast-forward two days after the first test disaster. We all got together again—this time with our parents—in the big meeting room by the apartments where we live.

"See? I told you she was a GEEN-ius!" Tag looked

at everyone as if I'd just hand-built a new faster-than-light space shuttle.

All I'd done was hook up a simple 3-D holo-vid projector to my drone. That, and add a few spare parts. But yes, I had my drone pretty much fixed. It even floated now, more or less the way it was supposed to. My teacher, Ms. Dos, was going to love it.

And now the other AstroKids wanted to show their parents what a great idea it would be to have Zero-G stop by to film their concert. My holo-vid projector would show everybody how "good" the band was.

"Are you sure this is going to work?" Miko whispered in my ear.

BG. I nodded. (That's a **B**ig **G**rin. And VBG is a **V**ery **B**ig **G**rin.)

Of course it was going to work. Just slip the little silver holo-vid disk into a slot in the drone's side. A pair of green lights blinked on the side of the drone.

"I'm not so sure we want to see this, ah, music group." Mr. Bright, Buzz's dad, sat down next to Mrs. Bright. They were talking to my mom, and the adults didn't look too sure.

Buzz stood up in front. "Okay, thanks, everybody, for taking your lunchtime to see our test concert."

Buzz was always really good in front of people.

Everybody waited, even the grown-ups.

"We figured if you saw what Zero-G looked like, maybe you'd let us invite them to the station. They're really nice guys, and they have good songs, too . . . about spaceships and funny animals and stuff. Nothing weird. Lots of kids like their music."

"And just think," Tag chimed in, "if they filmed a concert here, we'd be famous!"

"Don't count on it, boys," said Mr. Bright.

Buzz gave us his own BG and went on. "Thanks, DeeBee, for fixing up a holo-vid projector so we could see this." He waved a hand at my drone, which floated in the middle of the room, ready. "Go for it."

"Play disk," I told my drone. I had it set up for voice command.

The lights on my holo-vid projector started flashing blue-green. That was a good sign. But nothing else happened.

"Is it working?" Mr. Bright asked.

"Play DISK," I said again.

"Maybe you should say please," suggested Tag.

I sighed. "I don't think saying please is going to help, Tag."

"Just try it."

"All right, *please* play disk. There, see? Nothing. I told you that—"

Suddenly the drone quivered a little bit. A pink light flashed through the projector eye. A 3-D figure popped into the air in front of us.

"Ladies and gentlemen" came a recorded voice, "I present to you . . . Zero-Geeeeeee!"

3 Mir Did It

So there they were: Zero-G, in their red, white, and blue sparkly jump suits. No way you'd ever get *me* to wear something like that. But we watched the five of 'em play on a floating stage. They seemed very good at hopping up and down.

One teeny problem: They were only about half size, about a meter tall. That's the way my holo-vid projector made it look. It was the best I could do with the parts I could find.

Even so, we could hear how the crowd at the concert cheered and stomped and clapped.

QUESTION 04:

I'm having a hard time imagining what you mean by "holo-vid projector."

ANSWER 04:

Well, it's almost like being there, except you can see through the people. That's what holo-vid pictures are like. You can see all the way around them, from any side, but they're kind of see-through, too.

Anyway, the band started belting out one of their hits. Red and green and blue laser lights washed all over them. I wished I could plug my ears without looking too nerdy.

"Nice job, DeeBee." My dad was talking about the way I hooked up the holo-vid projector to the drone.

"Thanks." I was still nervous about this whole thing. The parts I'd used hadn't quite fit together.

"Snurple toothpaste (oooh-oooh) zapped from Mars . . ." the lead singer yelled out the words. "Jelly lasers (yeah-yeah) aim at chorpoo stars . . ."

Or something like that. It was kind of hard to understand the words, especially with all the oooh-ooohs and yeah-yeahs.

Buzz's mom frowned, and she wasn't the only one. In fact, all the adults looked as if they had awful headaches. The laser lights were getting brighter and wilder.

"Now, Daphne . . ." My mother shifted in her chair and put her hands over her ears.

She and my father were the only ones who ever

called me Daphne (my real name) and not DeeBee. (Which stands for Database, as in, computer. Kind of geeky, but I like it way better than *Daphne.*)

"Do you think you can turn it down a bit?" Mom continued.

Believe me, by that time I'd already thought of turning it down. Way down. As in, off. I tried every voice command I could think of. "Down volume!"

The yeah-yeahs got louder.

"Hush!"

No luck. We plugged our ears.

So how about, "Not so loud, PLEASE!"

Still nothing, except "oooh-oooh!"

My drone just wasn't listening; it was rocking with the music, grooving to the beat. So there was only one way to stop the wild Zero-G show: Pull out the holo-disk.

But when I tried, *yeowch!* I yanked my hand away from a blue spark.

"I'm sorry, Daphne," said the drone. "I'm afraid I can't let you do that."

"What's going on?" whispered my dad. Like I told you, he works on electro-whazzits and drones all day. So if he didn't know what was going on . . . Not good.

Tag didn't even notice; he was too busy watching.

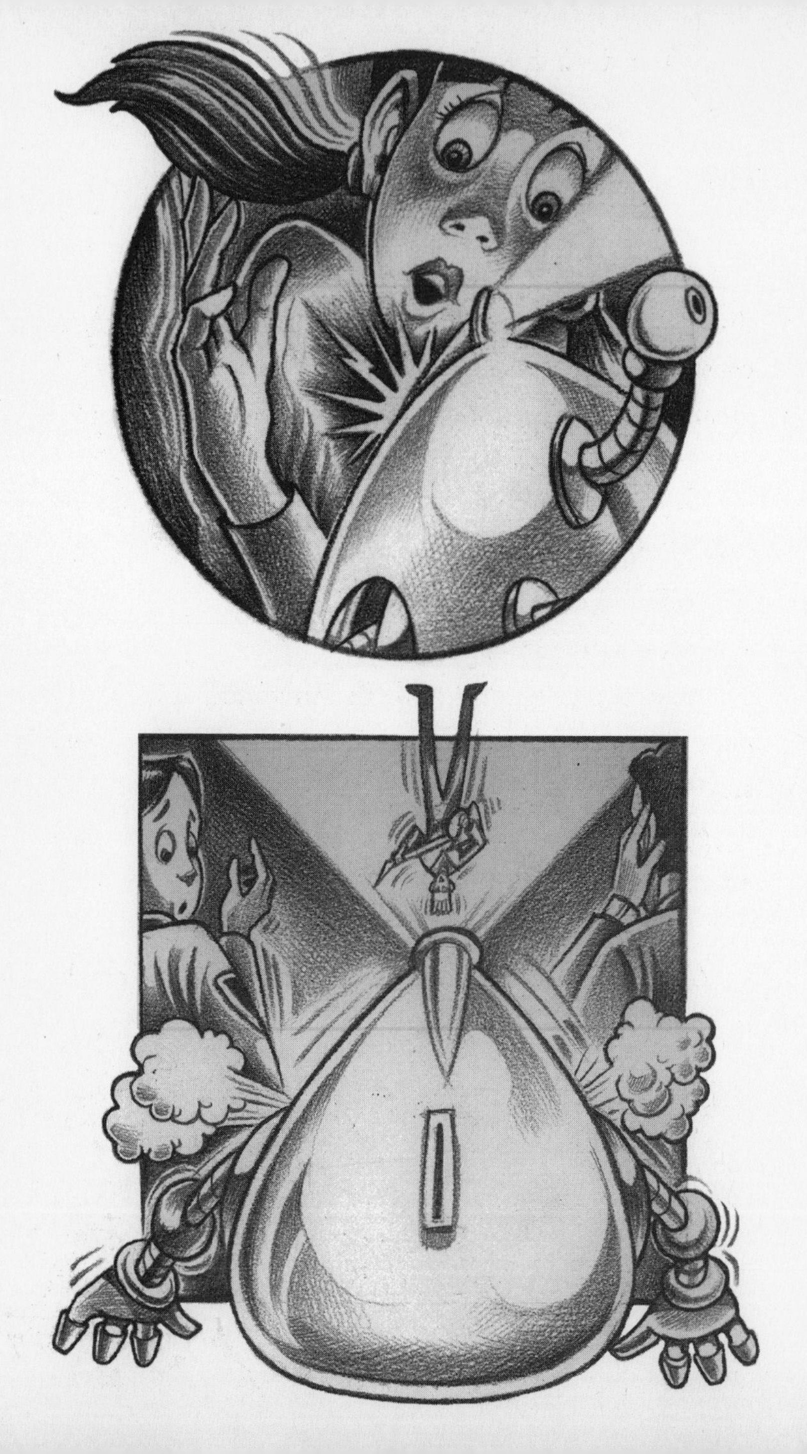

"Here comes the good part," he told us. "Check it out!"

Thanks, Tag. While I was being attacked by my drone, he was busy watching the Zero-G lead singer climbing the ceiling. The hologram man was having a great time hanging upside down in a pair of very cool—and very expensive—antigravity sneakers.

By now, the drone was really shaking. The holo-vid started flickering.

Suffering satellites!

"Shut it down!" said my dad.

Now the projector was flashing red. The holo-people turned purple, then green. They looked very sick.

Everyone jumped up—my parents, Buzz's parents . . .

"What's that smell?" Miko asked.

Uh-oh! There was now smoke coming out of cracks in the drone.

Not good.

Finally, the holo-band vaporized. *Poof!* The meeting room went dark.

This holo-show was over.

"Umm . . . lights on," Buzz voice-commanded the

lights. The walls in the room glowed with soft light again.

My poor drone lay shivering on the floor.

"Not again," I groaned. This time, the drone was toast for sure. Not just stepped on like before. I stood there, staring at it.

The door swooshed open.

"Oh dear! Are we having problems again?" It was Mir, the son of our station commander. Perfect timing.

"As if you didn't know." I straightened my hair and tried to look as if nothing were wrong. "But we can handle it."

Call it a feeling. A guess. But I'd say there was a total, 101-percent chance Mir Chekhov was behind this blowup.

QUESTION 05:

Why would you think that? Mir just walked in to see what happened.

ANSWER 05:

That's what it looks like. But you remember what happened in *The Great Galaxy Goof*, don't you? No? Read it and find out! Mir's a sneaky one. . . .

4 Big Secret

"Wait a minute!" Mir held up his hands like he was giving up a fight. "You don't think *I* had anything to do with this?"

I don't know, but that sounded like a guilty thing to say. I picked up my dead drone and held it in my arms. It was still warm and steaming. Me, I was steaming, too, but for a different reason.

"I'm not saying anything else," I snapped back and started pushing my way out of the room. I didn't want to say something rude. "All I know is my drone's auto-control function disengaged just before Mir showed up."

"In English, DeeBee." Tag stepped on my heel as I tried to hurry down the hall, back to the workshop. "You always start talking funny when you're mad."

"She means her drone went wacko just before Mir showed up," said Buzz. "Right, DeeBee?"

I was afraid I'd maybe start crying if I tried to say

anything else. And I really did not want to cry. I bit my lip instead.

"DeeBee, wait!" Mir ran up behind us. "You think I was playing another bad joke?"

"Well?" I stopped, and everybody in the parade piled into me.

"Well . . . I wasn't. Not this time."

"Hmm." I turned around to look at Mir. My mistake. Because when you look at Mir, you almost can't help smiling. No matter what. He has crazy, curly blond hair and a grin that won't stop. A VBG.

"Besides," he said, "wait until you hear."

"Hear what?" I asked.

Mir kept grinning.

"I'll tell you when I can," he whispered. "But not out where people can hear us."

I let Mir help me carry the dead drone back down the hall to the shop. Okay, so I think I believed him. Maybe he hadn't done anything to disengage the drone's auto-control funct—I mean . . . uh . . . make it go wacko.

But what had? And what was Mir's big secret?

"That was sure a bad accident," Buzz sighed as we walked down the hall. "Our parents will *never* let Zero-G come to the station now."

"Not after *that* show," agreed Miko.

"So much for being famous," said Tag.

Famous-shmaymus. All I knew was that my school project was trashed. Fried. Scrambled. Cooked.

And so was I, if I didn't figure a way out of this mess. Even worse, my friends probably blamed me for the mini-concert blowing up.

"I'm sure it wasn't your fault, DeeBee." Mir tried to help with the drone as we stepped through the swooshing doors into the shop. "Drones are hard to figure out."

"Yeah," piped up Tag, "but my sister's a GEE—"

I stopped him with a pleading look: *Please don't say that again, Tag. Please.*

For once, he got the message and zipped his lips.

See, I had wanted to make sure things would be different when my family came to *CLEO*-7. Back on Earth, kids would always call me *Brainiac* or *Megabrain* or *Orbit-head*. And then they would act as if I had some kind of deadly Martian disease. After a while, they would find someone else to play with.

My best guess was they were afraid of me for being smart.

Here on *CLEO*-7, they weren't calling me names . . . yet. Pretty soon they would, though. Especially if my brother kept blabbing to everybody that I was a "GEEN-ius."

I'm not. People just think I am. And that drives me crazy! I like riding space skis and chasing comets and eating pizza with extra moon cheese. Just like everybody else.

I'm just an average girl!

Okay, so I don't much like Zero-G. But I do like having fun. Just give me a chance! I'd even thought of acting dumb. I thought maybe kids would like me better if I wasn't so smart.

"So you know what happened to your drone, right, DeeBee?" Buzz asked me. We stood around staring at the pile of space junk on the shiny steel work table.

"How would I know for sure?" I shrugged my shoulders. "I'm no genius."

I had a pretty good idea, though. Something in the first-level memory config . . . Oh, sorry. There I go again. I mean, the old parts I found for the holo-vid projector probably didn't quite fit the drone's parts. They worked for a while, but then they got overloaded.

Too much. Poof. It was my fault and no one else's.

"You can fix it, though, right?" Miko asked in her soft voice.

By that time, I had the cover off and took a look inside.

It wasn't a pretty sight.

5 Chocolate Helps Me Think

I could see what had happened when we pulled off my drone's cover. The bubble memory wasn't bubbling anymore. Things were melted that shouldn't have been. It smelled like dead plastic.

Very dead plastic.

Not good.

"Don't worry," said Mir, dusting off his hands. "It doesn't matter."

Easy for him to say. He didn't have a project to turn in to Ms. Dos the day after tomorrow. His life didn't depend on it.

"What do you mean, it doesn't matter?" Buzz asked.

Mir looked awfully pleased with himself. "I can tell you everything tomorrow night. I promise."

"Oh, come on," Buzz dared him. "You can tell us now."

But Mir wouldn't budge. He just smiled.

Boys! It wouldn't be so bad if they could help me

fix my drone. But there wasn't much chance of that.

Fast-forward to the dining room the next morning. We were all sitting around eating breakfast. Don't ask if I'd fixed my drone. (I hadn't.) But at least we finally found out what Mir was talking about.

The big secret.

"Attention, please, a special announcement." A hologram of the station commander's head popped up above each of the floating tables. Just like it would have with my wrist interface, only bigger. Everyone stopped eating to listen to Mir's dad.

"We're going to have some very special visitors today," said the commander. He looked around the dining room. I mean, his hologram did. It was very life-like, right down to the dark eyes, the heavy eyebrows, and the curly hair. "Thanks to my son, Mir, a group of galaxy-famous musicians is coming to visit us here on *CLEO-7*."

I looked over at Mir. He was wearing his VBG.

Here it comes.

The hologram smiled, too, as if he could hear the hum-buzz of excited people in the dining room.

"It's . . ." he began, then paused. "It's . . ."

Huh?

The station commander bent over to listen to someone whisper in his ear.

"Ah yes. Zero-G is the name of the band," he said. "And they're on their way to play here at our station. I hear they're going to record part of their vid-concert right here, too. So wear your best uniforms! More details later. Commander Chekhov out."

Everyone under eighteen went crazy with whoopwoos and whistling and clapping. Zero-G, the Gravity Groove Tour, 2175, coming to *CLEO-7*! Wow. I thought I heard some of the parents groan, though.

My mother touched my arm. "Daphne, how did you. . . ?"

"I didn't have anything to do with it, Mom. Honest."

I looked over to the other side of the dining room. About fifteen kids had crowded around Mir. He was eating it up. (The attention, not the breakfast.) Even Tag, Miko, and Buzz were slapping him on the back and giving him the galaxy salute. You know, where you hook little fingers and shake.

"It was Mir, I guess."

I knew I should have gone over there, too, and

acted excited like the rest of the AstroKids. I should have been a good sport.

But I just couldn't.

I thought of my wasted drone instead. And I felt kind of bad—pretending to like Zero-G, when I really couldn't stand them.

But something else still wasn't right. I just wasn't sure yet what it was.

So I wondered. Okay, I stewed about it. How had Mir done it? How had he talked Zero-G into coming to our little station? And why didn't he tell us before?

"Hey, DeeBee." A navtech named Andy Omega leaned across a table. He was a friend of my dad's. "How's your drone project doing? Best in the class, right?"

I looked past Andy's shoulder to the view windows. Hadn't he heard?

"It's toast." I tried to sound casual, as if I ruined my drone and flunked school every day.

"No. Really?"

"Really." I nodded. "I think I plugged two wrong circuits together."

"Tough break," he told me. "You should've kept a better 'ion' it."

Normally, I would have totally cracked up at Andy's

joke. But all I could think about was how Ms. Dos would break into orbit when she found out what I'd done.

"WHAT?" she would scream. Her double-tall purple bouffant hairdo would shake with anger. She'd look down her nose at me, cross her arms, and breathe fire. The other kids would sniggle. I could just imagine. "What did you do, donate your brain to science before you were done using it? You fail! You flunk! You're finished!"

Any way you looked at it, it would be ugly. I shivered.

"DeeBee?" Andy snapped me out of my nightmare.

"Oh. Sorry. I was just—"

"Don't sweat it. I've done the same thing. You should have seen the time when we sent out the Pluto probe, and . . ."

Andy had lots of stories about things that blew up, or remote-control planet explorer probes that crashed. Didn't make me feel much better, though. He didn't know Ms. Dos the way I did. But he was trying to cheer me up, which was nice.

I stared out the view port at the stars while he talked. I wondered if God had another planet we could move to. Anyplace far away from Ms. Dos would be fine. Just an asteroid, maybe. Nothing fancy. Whenever I look out the view ports, it always hits me how big God must be to make so many stars, so many planets, so many—

"DeeBee, are you listening?"

"Oh, what?" I shook my head. "No—yes, I mean . . . I guess I just need to think."

Yeah, right. What I needed was an escape. Or at least a good walk around the big, curving rim of the station. So I excused myself and stopped by the digital food copier on my way out of the dining room. I punched a couple of lighted yellow buttons and stuck my hand below the slot.

"Chocolate, please," I told the DFC. Maybe having it serve up my favorite brain food would help me think.

I stood there for a minute, waiting for my chocolate. Trying to come up with some way out of this mess.

But . . . speaking of mess, I guess my mind started wandering. Because when I looked down, I saw something dark and warm oozing all over my hand.

Chocolate. Only not the solid kind I expected.

"Oh man," I groaned. A brown river of sticky, gooey chocolate syrup ran down the wall, all over my shoes, and all over the floor. Everywhere!

Could it get any worse?

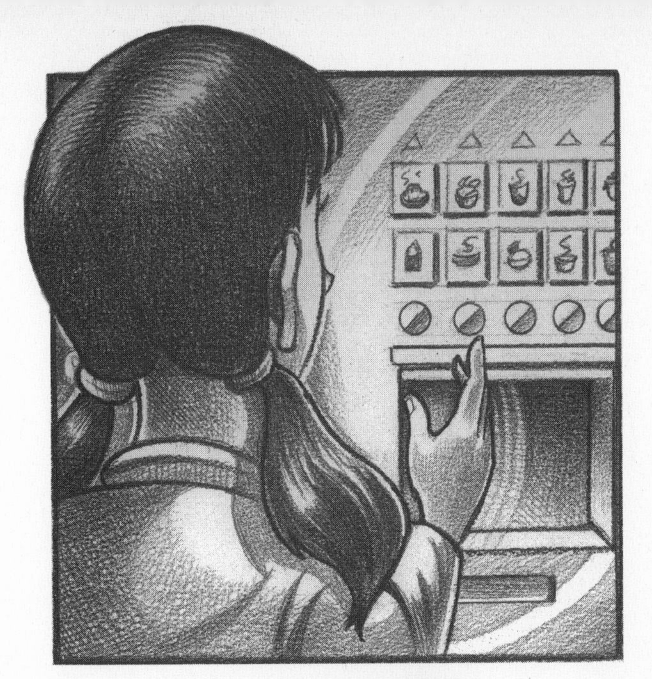

6 No Fair!

Yeah, things were getting a little weird around *CLEO-7*.

Did I say *a little* weird?

Wrong.

I meant *a lot* weird, and getting weirder all the time. For those of you who are keeping score . . .

The DeeBee Ortiz Top Three Weird Thing List

- Weird Thing 01: First my drone melts down. I already told you about my teacher, Ms. Dos, so you understand my life is over.
- Weird Thing 02: We find out Zero-G is coming here to film a concert. I still wondered how it happened. After all, *CLEO-7* is *not* the center of the universe.
- Weird Thing 03: My parents sit me and Tag down

in our den for a family meeting after dinner that night. I knew it was a family meeting because Dad cleared his throat and said, "Kids, we need to talk about something."

Now, if you've ever been through a family meeting, sometimes they're great. We had one before deciding to come to *CLEO-7*.

But then there are times you want to morph into a puddle of spilled water, slosh under the chair, and drip into the heating tube. Anything to get out of there. A long time ago in a galaxy far, far away would be just perfect.

This was one of those times.

"Tell me I'm dreaming." My little brother gasped, fell on the floor, and pretended he was dying. "He's coming here today? The same day as Zero-G?"

My dad rubbed his forehead. Tag hadn't quite learned yet that when Dad rubs his forehead, you keep quiet. And you don't pretend to die.

"Yes, Theodore. And you can get up off the floor now. Philip is your cousin, and you will treat him as a special guest. Understood?"

"But—"

Tag sat up while Dad went on.

"And since your cousin grew up in a mining camp on the moon, he's never known our side of the family. We expect you both to be very hospitable."

Grew up in a mining camp on the moon? Suffering satellites! Does he come complete with a bagful of rocks?

"How can I be hospital," whined Tag, "when we don't even *know* this guy?"

"Hos-*pit*-able," Dad corrected him.

"Ho-*SPIT*-able," repeated Tag.

"Watch it, Tag." I covered my face from the spray. Maybe Tag didn't know what *hospitable* meant, as in, having to be friendly to weird relatives who all of a sudden visit you at your space station and ruin your life.

But he brightened up, as if he had an idea. "So . . . he'll want to go to the Zero-G concert with us, right?"

"I'm sorry, no." Mom shook her head. "Uncle Harmonic, Philip's father, has asked us if we would help Philip put on a little recital for us instead. Naturally, your father and I agreed."

Tag's jaw dropped. A recital?

Mom explained some more. This time she was wearing her famous you're-going-to-love-this-and-boy-is-it-good-for-you smile. Last time I saw that smile, she was giving us our new chore list.

"Philip is an honor student at the Lunar Conservatory of Music. That's a special music school on the moon. He's a wonderful violinist. So—"

I gulped.

Tag launched. "But that's not fair!" My little brother sputtered like a shuttle on its last fuel cell. "We can't miss the Zero-G concert just because, because . . ."

"That's enough, Theodore." My father was *really* rubbing his forehead now.

Actually, I almost felt sorry for Tag. He looked up at me for help. *Sorry, pal.*

"But all the rest of the AstroKids are going to be there." Tag didn't know when to stop. "This is the event of the century. I'll just *die* if we miss it."

"You won't die," my mother said. No doubt she still remembered the holo-vid concert we put on for them. Remember when Zero-G blew up my drone and our eardrums? I'll bet she was thinking a nice, quiet violin recital would be just the ticket.

Maybe she was right. I was pretty sure I knew what a violin was. I'd seen one in an e-book once.

QUESTION 06:

Did you say e-book? What in the galaxy is an e-book?

ANSWER 06:

My friends and I still have books in 2175. But also e-books, which are big, bendy tablets with a flat screen. Download whatever you want to read in about three milliseconds. Want to learn about the past? No problem. How to build a space scooter? Zippidee-doo-dah. Where to find nummy snail farms on Venus? Uh, even that. E-books are like old-fashioned computers, only better.

"You haven't said anything, Daphne." My father looked at me, his eyebrows raised.

I looked from Tag to my parents. On the one hand, my AstroKid friends were all excited about Zero-G coming to the station. Just like Tag, or more. And I was one of the AstroKids, after all.

Or I hoped I was.

On the other hand, my parents wanted us to be hospitable to cousin Philip, no matter how odd he turned out to be.

Headache! I started to rub my forehead, too, just like my dad.

"I think . . ." I began, but I wasn't sure how I was going to finish.

Doop-doop! My father's wrist interface alarm sounded just then.

Yesss. I kept a straight face. Just in time.

"Hello?" Dad checked his wrist. Up popped the head of Commander Chekhov.

"Carlos, sorry to call you when you're off duty," said the commander. "But we have a shuttle coming in with that Zero-G group, and—"

"Already?" Dad asked.

"A little early, right." Commander Chekhov nodded. "But I'm calling you because the doors to shuttle hangar 01 are acting up. Can you run to the hub and take a look?"

"On my way," promised my dad, and he headed for the door.

"I'm sorry," my father told us. "We'll have to finish this talk later. But remember what we said about being *hospitable.* Right, Tag?"

Tag nodded, and Dad hurried out to fix the shuttle hangar doors. I followed him through the gardens. We turned to go up through one of the passageways to the middle of the station. That's the hub, where the big shuttle garages are. Dad's interface was crackling with new messages the whole time.

"Ten minutes until they're landing. Can they fit in shuttle hangar 02 instead of 01?"

I took a deep breath and got ready to be *hospitable* to the silliest, hottest band in the solar system.

7 Where ARE We?

Tag must have called the other AstroKids—and maybe everybody else on the station besides! By the time I got to the hub, there was already a line of people wanting to get into shuttle hangar 01. Some of them were holding colored signs that read *Welcome Zero-G!* or *CLEO-7 Rocks!*

TCFW. Too Cute For Words.

Or, as Tag would say, EMWIV. Excuse Me While I Vomit. But that's really rude, and he knows I hate the *v* word.

So I just strolled past the crowd, real slowly, real cool. I just wanted to see if anyone knew they were all waiting outside the wrong place. When no one was looking, I slipped past them and through the sliding door marked *Shuttle Hangar 02*.

Just as I thought. Nobody was there, except a couple of techs behind the see-through wall in front of the controls. I waved at them and found a safe place to watch the big doors open up.

I didn't have long to wait. In about two minutes, the door behind me sealed. Red lights started to flash. I was safe in the viewing area. You sure didn't want to be out on the shuttle-bay floor when those doors opened. *Whoosh!* You'd be sucked right out into space. Majorly not good.

It didn't happen, of course, and a beautiful silver shuttle nosed in as soon as the huge garage doors opened up. It had *Zero-G* painted in big, bright red curvy letters on the side. I was in the right place.

Almost before the doors were closed, air pumped back in. *Phhissh!* The big space bird clamped onto its docking legs.

"Welcome to *CLEO*-7," I whispered from my safe place. The shuttle's side door opened, and I waited to see what would happen.

First, a couple of fuzzy heads peeked out the shuttle door. Like, "Where are we?" They looked all rumpled—as if they had been drooling and were just waking up.

One of them asked how long they were stopping for repairs. The other said maybe only a few hours. Or maybe longer. Just long enough to figure out what was

the Zero Gs
the Zero Gs

wrong with their laser-map system. Then they'd be leaving right away.

That's about when the hallway door behind me finally zooped open. Stampede! All those people who had been waiting in the wrong place spilled inside. Someone screamed, but not like she was in pain. This was an I-can't-believe-I'm-in-the-same-room-as-ZERO-G! scream.

Remember, we're in the hub of a space station. And the hub doesn't have the same gravity as the rest of the station. Things pretty much float. That's why the space shuttles unload here. It's easier for them to just drift in, rather than try to catch up with the spinning part of the station.

Anyway, you can imagine what happened when this mess of people all tried to crowd in. They were floating and bouncing all over the place. Of course, everyone wanted to get close to the Zero-G guys.

"Would you sign my arm?" one of the girls asked a guy who came out of the shuttle.

Puh-leez. What a dumb old custom. Still, the Zero-G guys smiled and signed everything people brought them. Music disks, shirts, whatever. I thought it was very odd.

In the middle of it all, someone pushed a battered

old silver trunk out the side of the shuttle. It might have been heavy, except that things were almost weightless here in the hub.

"Oooh," squealed one of the girls. She noticed the guy with the trunk, too. "Which one are you?"

"I'm Ph-philip Harmonic." The teen looked confused. He wasn't very big. Not much older than me, either. "B-but my friends call me Phil. Which one are you?"

"Phil?" The other girl scratched her head. "You're not in Zero-G."

No, he wasn't. He was my cousin. *Suffering satellites!* I rubbed my forehead.

Phil looked kind of klutzy, and his hair stood straight up in back. A corner of his trunk hit the side of the shuttle door, and the top snapped open.

"Uh-oh," said Phil, and he stumbled out after it.

We spent the next few minutes chasing Phil's junk. And I do mean junk. Mostly socks and underwear and stuff, but also a couple of odd-looking wooden boxes with long handles, and . . .

"My violins," he told me. He set them back into the trunk the way you would a baby.

"You play those things?"

"Me?" He grinned and nodded. "You bet. I may

not know the d-difference between a particle beam and a bubble memory. But I like music. Phil Harmonic, the Music Nerd."

As I shook his hand, I wondered if his parents knew what they were doing when they named their baby Philip.

"How did you get a ride with . . . *them*?" I asked.

"Oh, right." He looked back at the shuttle. There was that grin again. "We met at the conservatory, before they were kicked—I mean, before they left to start their band."

"But you're friends?"

"Sure. Just watch out for old Rufus Trapezoid. He's a grouch!"

Rufus who? Who was that?

"The manager. He takes care of the band's business."

Oh. I took one side of the big trunk. That's when a smallish, red-faced man pushed by us and stepped off the shuttle. I guessed that would be Rufus Trapezoid. A couple of leftover fans were still waiting.

"We're, like, soooo excited you're going to do a concert for us!" a girl squealed and blocked the man's way. "This is, like, soooo kewl." She was, like, almost foaming at the mouth.

"Can I, like, be in the holo-vid, too?" squeaked another girl.

I thought I was, like, going to be ill. Maybe Tag was right about EMWIV.

"Concert? Holo-vids?" The man frowned. His cheeks lit up, supernova bright. (A supernova is a majorly bright star.) "You girls are dreaming. This is the *last* place anyone would do a concert. *Especially* Zero-G."

The *last* place?

Everyone turned to Mir.

8 Not in the Contract

"Listen." Mir held up his hands and caught his breath. "I'm really sorry, okay?"

Sorry? You should have seen the guy squirm when everybody was staring at him back in shuttle hangar 02. And I'll tell you, Mir can run pretty fast when he wants to get away. We didn't catch up with him until we reached the shop.

Sorry, he said?

"But you intentionally obfuscated the factualities!" I told him.

Meaning, big boo-boo.

Extreme error.

Mix-up to the max.

"Do you mean he lied on purpose?" Miko wanted to make sure. She picked up a piece of my melted drone from the workbench.

"I did not lie." Mir looked around the shop, where we had decided we'd better hold a special AstroKids meeting. "I told you Zero-G was coming, and now they're here."

"But they're only here to get their shuttle fixed," I argued. "That's what I heard them saying."

"What do they know?" Mir shrugged.

"I'm just telling you what I heard, Mir. Part of their shuttle's laser-map system is missing. And that old Rufus Trapezoid is pretty steamed about it. He's pretty steamed about having to stop here at all."

"Okay," said Mir, "but—"

"So they didn't come here for a concert, did they? They're not going to film a holo-vid, either. Right?"

This time Mir didn't answer, and I went on. I felt like a winning lawyer making my case in court. I started pacing the shop.

"So here's what happened."

DeeBee Ortiz, Space Lawyer in Action

- "Fact 01: You found out from your dad they were stopping here for repairs, on the way to Mars. (Jab finger at suspect.)
- "Fact 02: They were coming here anyway. (Cross arms.)

- "Fact 03: But you made it sound as if *you* were the one who brought them here." (Stand up straight.)

Case closed, I thought.

Right?

"Uh . . ." Mir stared at his green gripper shoes.

"But you never even *talked* to them, did you?"

"Maybe not in the past few days."

"Explain 'few' days."

"Well . . . maybe not lately."

"Did you ever?"

"I was going to."

"Sure. You stood up in front of everybody with all that lah-dee-dah talk. You let us think you were such a great guy for getting Zero-G to come here. Isn't that right?"

Finally, Mir looked up at me.

Whoops. I didn't expect to see tears in his eyes.

"Look, I'm sorry it turned out this way." His voice shook. "I don't even really like Zero-G's music. I was just trying to do something so people would . . . like me better."

Ouch.

Why did this sound so familiar? Maybe because it was something *I* could be saying—if I told the truth.

No one said anything. And all of a sudden, I didn't feel like a lawyer in a court. I just felt like a 1CH.

A **F**irst-**C**lass **H**ypocrite. You know. Someone who believes one way but acts another.

I'd pretended to like Zero-G, too. I'd been afraid nobody would like me if I didn't say I liked the group.

Just like Mir.

I didn't quite know what else to say. But when the shop door swooshed open, I thought it would be a good excuse to change the subject. We turned to see who it was.

"Come here, you crazy mutt!" shouted a man. It sounded like Rufus Trapezoid.

A blur of fur raced by with something in its mouth. Next came Rufus, limping and huffing. I got the feeling he wasn't going to enter the Intergalaxy Olympics any time soon.

"What was that?" Tag asked.

"Beats me," Miko said, "but let's find out!"

We ran after her.

"Over here!" cried Tag. A minute later, he had the dog cornered next to a pile of half-finished drones.

We were there in a zip. Rufus Trapezoid was still looking on the other side of the shop. I could hear him stomping his feet and muttering.

"Here, little guy." Buzz got down on all fours and crawled up to the dog. It was a weird-looking animal, but really cute. Maybe half chihuahua and half beagle, with a blaze of white fur on the head. It was wagging its tail like crazy, as if they were playing a great game. And it had a small black box in its mouth.

"What've you got there, pal?" I got down on the floor next to Buzz, trying to get a look at the puppy's strange box.

"THERE he is!" Rufus yelled, finally coming up behind us.

The dog scrambled behind a metal drone body. (Who could blame him?) I crawled closer, under a shelf, and whispered nice things to keep the mutt from running away.

"Nice boy," I told him. "You're not going to bite me, right?"

I reached out slowly. The dog stared at me. At least if he was going to bite, he'd have to drop the black box first.

Slowly. One more centimeter. Got it! The box . . . and the dog. He still wasn't letting go.

"Don't tell me this is the missing part from the laser-map system?" I pointed to the box held between my hand and the mutt's teeth.

"Bad, bad dog!" Rufus had fire in his eyes, and the stubborn pooch wisely gave up.

"It's a little soggy." I checked out the box before I handed it over. It looked like part of a laser-map system, all right. About the size of a sandwich, and full of electro-circuits. "But I don't think the teeth marks hurt anything. He looks like a sweet puppy."

" 'Sweet' is not the word." Rufus grabbed the box and held it up in the air, away from the dog. "He's a thief."

The dog wagged his tail and stood up on his hind legs. Yeah, we were talking about him.

"Where'd he come from?" I asked.

"Venus Base 12." Rufus picked up the dog in his free hand and turned to go. "And I should have left him there. But a fan gave him to us. You should try traveling with a dog for a couple of light-years. They want to stop and sniff every asteroid."

The dog wiggled. And I'm sure he winked at me.

A dog? Winking his eye? Hey, I'm telling you, that's what it looked like.

"Uh, I guess I should thank you, kid," Rufus said as he left us. "Maybe now we'll be able to get out of here."

"Great," I said. Whoops. Was that the right thing to say?

"And . . ." He stopped before he left us. He looked as if he were in pain. "I . . . guess I owe you one. So if there's anything I can do for you, just let me know."

I'm not sure if he really meant what he said. But since he mentioned it, maybe there was something. . . .

9 Poof!

No, it wasn't "in the contract" to play at a little station like *CLEO-7*. So Rufus Trapezoid reminded us they were doing us a Big Fat Favor to change their plans and put on a show here.

More than once he reminded us.

The guys in Zero-G were on their way to the Mars colony, after all, where there were bazillions of adoring fans waiting for the Gravity Groove Tour, 2175. EMWIV.

Actually, I've been there once. It has three underground cities. Very cool trains that zip all over the place. And since Mars gets *very-very-very* cold, they pump heat up from the middle of the planet. Ultra awesome.

Compared to Mars, then, *CLEO-7* is a tiny village. A quick pit stop on the space highway.

But Rufus Trapezoid didn't have to be such a grump about staying here. He didn't have to complain so much. I was listening as I helped fix up the sound system in our biggest meeting room. The main sound tech had gone to get more parts.

Actually, I was the only one there, except for the five Zero-G boys. But I had to leave in a couple of hours to meet Phil, Tag, and the rest of the family. No concert for me. Remember? Phil's recital? Thrillsville.

"We play just three songs tonight, right?" asked the lead extar player. The others called him A.C. He looked like he was the oldest, maybe nineteen.

"Yup. Only three," said the other extar guy. I think his name was Zowie. "That's what Rufus promised the kids."

As for the rest of Zero-G? Here they are. . . .

- Zoey played a zeeboard. It's a floating black board kind of thing with red-, white-, and green-colored buttons on the top. At least, I *think* he played it. Either that, or the computer did.
- Justout pounded on a floating ten-head electro-sensor drum set. *Ka-POW-a-pung, pang, pong!*
- Kriz, the fifth one, bounced around a lot. I guess he sang, too.

QUESTION 07:

Wait a minute. Extars? What are extars?

Answer 07:

> Extars are sort of like those electric guitars people used to play, only way different. Extars have a see-through triangle body that changes colors. Plus twenty-four titanium strings, and laser diodes inside that give it a really cool sound.

"Well, the sooner we get off this wreck, the better." Rufus stepped into the room as the band tuned up.

Wait a minute, I thought. *"Wreck"?* Maybe our drones didn't always work the way they were supposed to. But "wreck"? *I don't think so.*

"Relax, Rufe, dude," said A.C. "The kids here are, like, totally cool."

Yeah, I thought. *Like, you tell him.*

"But what about that dog?" yelled Rufus. "I lock him in the shuttle; you boys let him out. He's driving me crazy, stealing things. He's the reason we're stuck here in the first place."

The Zero-G guys laughed as the dog flew down the shuttle steps. He touched down lightly at the bottom and bounced up again. Like an old-fashioned yo-yo. He was used to being near-weightless, for sure.

And for sure, he had something in his mouth again. Another black box? No, it was smaller this time.

"What does he have *now*?" Rufus grabbed at the dog and missed.

The others kept laughing.

"Just let him go, Rufe," said A.C. "He can't hurt anything. The laser-map system is fine now. And we've got work to do."

So they let him go. Rufus didn't like it, but they did.

Still, I wondered what the dog had found in the shuttle. I couldn't tell. He seemed to be making strange giggling noises.

"Ha-ha-ha," laughed a voice that seemed to come from the dog. It was tinny and hollow, and very faint. "Ha-ha-ha."

The dog, laughing? No way. That would be too weird. Anyway, he was suddenly nowhere to be seen. He must have found a place to hide with his new treasure.

"All right, fine." Rufus shrugged. "Let's do our sound check and get this over with."

That's when Mir, Buzz, and Miko came in to help.

"Aren't you still working on your drone project?" Buzz asked me.

"Did all I could." I shrugged and tried not to think

about what would happen to me the next day. "I ran out of parts. I'm history."

Since I couldn't work on the drone, I figured I could at least help work on the sound system. And I'm telling you, I did my best. But it must not have been good enough.

"Here, let me see that." Rufus moved in. Didn't shove me, exactly, but close. He took the controls and started punching buttons.

"I wouldn't do it that way," I told him. "We've had some problems lately. Had to use some spare parts that don't exactly—"

"No problem, kid." Rufus brushed me off. "I've done this a thousand times before."

"But your instruments don't quite match our system. You have to—"

"Yeah, yeah." Rufus just fiddled with the controls as if I didn't know what I was talking about.

"She can do it," said Miko.

"Yeah, Rufe, let her do it," A.C. agreed. "She knows the system on this station better than we do, dude."

"Speak for yourself." Rufus pointed at the band boys. "Now, crank it up. Let me hear how it sounds."

So A.C. and his friend Zowie began cranking up their extars.

And it sounded . . . Well, after a few minutes, I just had to plug my ears. Suffering satellites! Was I ever going to hear again? I kept an eye on the control board, watching the lights, expecting it to go *ka-poof.* But nothing happened.

At first.

Rufus poked more buttons. The screeching and pounding got louder and louder. I smelled something like . . . smoke?! I tried one last time to get through to him.

"It really can't take that kind of load, Mr. Trapezoid," I yelled and pointed at the controls. The board started to quiver and shake, and the overhead lights dimmed. What now?

He waved me off. "I'm telling you, kid, I know what I'm—"

Ka-POOF!

". . . doing."

10 Phil Harmonic's Idea

You have to know what happened next: the biggest light show you've ever seen.

Snap! Crackle! Pop!

Miko and Buzz hit the floor when yellow sparks showered out the front of the zeeboard. So did Mir.

Overload, for sure.

ZWAAAP! A blue flame licked out of A.C.'s extar.

"Dude!" He dropped it on the floor like a white-hot solar flare.

"Whoa!" cried the other band members. Their faces went as pale as the bright side of the moon. Rufus did a quick jig away from the sparks, but they just kept coming.

I don't think anybody was hurt. But, still, this was not good. I reached out and snapped off the control board's power before we fried the whole station.

What a mess! And it wasn't just the sparks. Fire alarms howled over our heads.

Ah-OO-gah! Ah-OO-gah!

Lights blinked. Everybody hollered. Station officials like my dad came running up to see what had happened. Even my cousin Phil dashed into the room to find out what was going on. He'd been on a tour of *CLEO-7* with my parents. Tag was right on his heels.

By that time, I'd grabbed an ion fire extinguisher. I figured I'd better do something—quick. Before this end of the station roasted!

Whooosh! First, I doused the zeeboard with my extinguisher. For a second, I couldn't see through the gray cloud. That was okay, but it turned the instrument into a frozen snow statue.

"The zeeboard!" complained Rufus. "No!"

Way too late. I gave it another quick shot, which iced it for sure.

The extars were already melted. At least they weren't flaming meteors anymore.

But you never know. I gave them a little *phoot* with the extinguisher, too. Just for good measure.

Twang!

And the twenty-four hot extar strings . . .

Tweng!

. . . snapped and curled . . .

Twing!

. . . when the cold fog . . .

Twong!

. . . hit 'em.

Twung!

"Dude!" said A.C. "That was extreme! Do it again."

I didn't think that was a good idea.

"Are you kids all right?" my dad wanted to know. We were. Fact is, everyone was okay . . . except Rufus. He was breathing enough for three people. And his cheeks could have passed for Martian tomatoes. For a second, I thought of cooling him down with a *phoot* from the fire extinguisher.

But no. His hair probably would have done the same thing as the extar strings. Definitely not a good idea.

"We're fine, Mr. Ortiz." Buzz got to his feet with a hand from cousin Phil.

"Easy for *you* to say, kid," Rufus Trapezoid sputtered. "But who's going to pay for this . . . this mess? The instruments. They're ruined."

He was right. But whose fault was that?

We all looked at each other.

"I tried to tell her not to . . . uh . . . push the system so much." Rufus noticed my father and pointed at me.

"I warned her not to turn it up so loud. But she just wouldn't listen."

No way! The words hit like a force-field torpedo. Rufus was blaming *me*?

Not to worry. My dad took one look at me, and I'm sure he knew better.

The Zero-G guys stared at their manager with their mouths open.

"That's not true!" Mir was the first one to say something. "DeeBee told *you* not to turn it up so loud. She tried to warn you. We saw the whole thing."

Just then I could have planted a big kiss on Mir's forehead. How do you like that? Mir, of all people, sticking up for me!

"Well, I—" Rufus sputtered. "Perhaps . . ."

I could tell this guy's thrusters were in full reverse. Thanks to Mir!

And Miko was nodding her head. She was on my side, too.

"All right, all right." My dad held up his hands like a referee in a fight. "Whatever happened, I'm sure it was an accident."

Yeah, but this was one supernova of an accident. And I knew what was coming next. . . .

"There will be no concert tonight!" announced

Rufus. "My boys can't play without their instruments. We're out of here."

So that was it. No concert. No filming the holo-vid. No being famous. Tag groaned—not that he was going to the concert anyway.

And not that being famous mattered to me. But I still felt pretty bad. What if it really was my fault? Or worse yet, what if people *thought* it was my fault?

After all, I was the one holding the fire extinguisher. And just look at those instruments! Dead. Done. History.

But the fried instruments must have given my cousin an idea. He leaned over and whispered in my ear.

What? Sure, it was wild and crazy, but maybe . . . right now anything was worth a try. I looked over at Phil and gave him a thumbs-up.

"Ah-HEM." Phil cleared his throat. "I don't s-s-suppose anyone would like to hear DeeBee's and my idea?"

Everyone looked at Phil Harmonic. Hey, it wasn't exactly *my* idea, but . . .

"It's not a bad idea, really," I told them.

Phil grinned at everybody, then said, "Because it means we can still have a concert tonight!"

YG2BK

You've seen frozen smiles before. When people don't really want to say what they're thinking? They're smiling. They're trying to be polite.

And that's what people did when cousin Phil said we could still have our concert.

But inside they were thinking, YG2BK.

You've Got To Be Kidding.

See, the Zero-G instruments were still smoking. And this is cousin Phil Harmonic, remember? The music nerd?

Well, fast-forward to that night, when we had at least half of *CLEO-7* packed into shuttle hangar 02. It's the biggest room in the station, after all. And they still had to clean up the meeting room. Just about everyone was wearing their gripper boots. That way, they wouldn't float away. (Although, a few people floated around, just for fun.)

The Zero-G shuttle was still in there, all fixed up, charged up, and ready to take off. We had set up a stage for the band right next to the shuttle, with laser lights and everything. Zero-G could leave right after the concert.

"Your attention, please!" Phil floated up in front and waved his hands. His hair still stuck up straight in back. And his old violin was kind of geeky. But with green and red lights washing over him, he actually looked sort of . . . cool. "Could I have your attention?" Phil continued.

Everyone hushed.

"The boys have asked me to thank you for making them f-feel so welcome."

Big cheers. Phil grinned.

"And I want to dedicate this set to DeeBee Ortiz and her brother, Tag, for doing so much to help us out!"

I didn't know he was going to say that. Can you say "embarrassed"?

But he was a typical boy. He didn't notice me blushing. "And now, *CLEO-7*, we have a special treat for you. My friends, Zero-Geeeeeee!"

That's when everybody lost it. You know, clapping, stomping, hollering . . .

But Tag just stared at Phil's instrument as our cousin tuned up and the five Zero-G guys took the stage.

"Where's the, uh, power source?" he hollered in my ear.

"No power source," I smiled. "It's all manual. That's how they made music hundreds of years ago."

"I don't believe it."

Believe it! Sure, Phil's violin was ancient. What, three hundred years old? But when he pulled a bow across the strings, he could sure make that old instrument sing!

The guys in Zero-G sang, too. And good old Phil—he had figured out their songs, just like that. So he played the tunes while they did the words. And guess what? I actually liked it!

So did everybody else. Pretty soon, we were all singing along. Even Commander Chekhov, standing off in the back, was moving his lips. (Two girls floating around with holo-cams got the whole thing on disk.)

"Snurple toothpaste (oooh-oooh) zapped from Mars . . ." A.C. yelled out the words this time. "Jelly lasers (yeah-yeah) aimed at chorpoo stars . . ."

I still wasn't sure about the words . . . but whatever.

"We're in the Gravity Groove Tour, 2175, holo-vid!" hollered Mir. He waved at the cameras and tried to hog the scene, until Miko told him to sit down, please.

Anyway, they got tons of pictures: Zero-G leaning together and singing without their instruments. Zero-G dancing and hopping in their dorky sparkle suits. Plus lots of close-ups of Phil playing his amazing violin. The cute dog even showed up on stage to howl along.

In between songs, Phil told jokes that made everyone LOL. (That's Laugh Out Loud.) Who would've thought?

But we loved every minute. And pretty soon, the Zero-G guys were finishing up the show. We wanted more.

By that time, even Ms. Dos was smiling and clapping. VBG. First time I'd ever seen her do that. Was she feeling okay? Maybe she'd caught a Martian bug of some kind. I tried to stay away from her . . . just in case.

But suffering satellites! Suddenly she was pushing her way through the crowd to see me. *Uh-oh.*

"Hey, DeeBee!" Phil yelled at me over the clapping and hooting. He waved for me to come over to the shuttle. Maybe he wanted to say good-bye.

If that's what he wanted, this was a strange time to

do it. But strange is good, especially with Ms. Dos on the prowl. I ducked through the crowd.

Inside the Zero-G shuttle, Phil had pried the top off an odd-looking, old blue plasma barrel. He started pulling things out to show me. As if it were Christmas or something.

“What’s all this?” I asked.

12 And Nuf, Besides

What *was* all this odd stuff in cousin Phil Harmonic's barrel?

I picked up a drone arm made from see-through green metal. Very weird, and probably very old. I could see all the wires and servos and circuits inside. And when I picked it up, it kind of jerked—the way your knee does when you tap it just right.

"Whoa!" I let go, and it floated off. "This thing's still powered up!"

" 'Armed' and dangerous." Phil grinned and fetched the floating part. "This was our great-grandfather's stuff, back on the moon. Experiments and drone parts, mostly."

"So how did you get it?" I asked.

"My dad was cleaning out our home pod. He thought I could make a great instrument from some of the parts. So he gave them all to me. But I have no idea what to do. See, I'm a musician, not a tekky."

I dug into the barrel again, just to see what else was there. Sensors, power supplies, memory chips . . . But then—ahh!—a pair of loose silicon eyeballs blinked at me. I pulled my hand back.

"A-actually," my cousin stuttered, "I think you should have it."

"No kidding?" I wondered if he was serious. "For me?"

"Unless you don't want it." He shrugged. "I'll just drag it all back to—"

"No! I mean, yes! Sure!"

I couldn't believe it! All these great parts. Even the eyeball lenses. Maybe I could find something to fix my drone project after all!

Who was I kidding? If I had about three more weeks, maybe. But by tomorrow morning? I didn't think so.

"What's wrong, DeeBee? Your parents said you were great with this kind of stuff."

"Oh, I don't know. . . ."

"Come on. I *am* talking to DeeBee the 'GEEN-ius,' am I not?"

"Well . . ." I sighed. Phil was a nice guy. But he didn't know what it was like to have everyone always call you that.

"There's nothing wrong with being smart, DeeBee, or good at different things. God gave us different gifts."

I thought about Phil playing his old violin, and telling jokes.

"I guess so." Maybe he was right. But I have to say it was a little strange to have this cousin tell me so. He smiled and waved at someone stepping in through the door behind me.

"Come in, come in!"

Uh-oh. I knew in a microsecond who it was. Yeah, I could smell Ms. Dos's perfume ("Passion of Pluto") a light-year away. I could hear her double-tall purple bouffant hairdo scrape along the low shuttle ceiling.

Suffering satellites!

"Miss Ortiz," she announced. "There you are."

I gulped. This was it. I was cornered.

"I've been looking all over for you," she went on. "You weren't in your lab today."

"No, ma'am, I—"

"Never mind. I hear your cousin brought you some rare drone parts."

How did everyone else know these kinds of things before I ever did?

"I . . . guess that's so, ma'am." I nodded and held my breath.

She looked at the plasma barrel and poked at a power supply. It went *phhyzzt*, and she pulled her hand back.

"Then I assume you'll need a few more weeks to complete your project?"

Did I hear her right? More time?

"Uh . . . yes, ma'am. That would—"

"Three more weeks, then. Will that be enough?"

Was I dreaming? Did she say *three weeks*? No problem!

"Yes, ma'am. Thank you, ma'am."

"Thank your cousin."

Just then the crowd clapped wildly. We looked out to see Zero-G coming back for one more song.

"That's my cue," said Phil. He grabbed his violin and skipped down the shuttle steps and onto the stage.

Again, everybody cheered. But nobody louder than me.

* * *

"Aren't you glad I brought them here?" Mir asked me. The Zero-G boys had just finished their encore and were taking bows. Even the dog bowed.

I just nodded. Yes, I was glad. Even though the way it all happened was a bit . . . weird.

"Your dog's pretty smart, Mr. Trapezoid," said Buzz.

"*My* dog?" Phil's violin playing must have softened up even grumpy old Rufus, because he said, "He's *your* dog now, kids. If you want him."

"Well . . ." My dad gave the dog a careful once-over, as if it might have brought Martian fleas to the station.

The dog winked at Dad. (I'm sure of it!)

"Hey, dudes, come here," whispered A.C. "Truth is, the poor mutt doesn't exactly . . . like Rufus. But he thinks you guys are, like, totally extreme. Why don't you keep him?"

All us AstroKids turned to look up at my dad.

He rubbed his forehead. I mean, *really* rubbed his forehead. But finally, he sighed and nodded.

So the strange dog was ours! But what would we call him?

"You're the smart one." Phil grinned at me. "You come up with a name."

"How about we call him Zero-G?" I figured the band guys would like that.

"Perfect," they said.

Miko thought maybe we could call him Zero for short, or maybe Z.

"My sister's a GEEN-ius," Tag told everyone. "But I guess she's *nuf*, too."

Nuf? Oh yeah. *Fun,* spelled backward.

For once, I didn't mind Tag and his silly backwards stuff. Neither did anyone else. We were too busy waving good-bye to Phil and his friends. And I can tell you that everyone was sorry to see them go. Even Ms. Dos blew them a kiss. (She must've thought no one was watching.)

But that wacko dog—you know, Zero-G? Call me crazy, but I had a feeling he was going to get us into a lot of *elbuort*.

You know, *trouble*!

RealSpace Debrief

* * *

The AstroKids Guide to Real (and Pretend) Trips to Mars

You remember how Zero-G was on their way to a concert on Mars. What's the big deal about Mars? Here's the scoop.

It's our closest planet. (Don't count the moon as a planet.) And when an Italian astronomer named Schiaparelli (shap-ah-RELL-ee) discovered lines on the surface in 1877, people started wondering. The lines looked just like canals. What if someone had dug the canals? That would mean . . . Yeah! Martians!

Schiaparelli helped start the Martian craze that's still going on today. Around 1900, an American named Percival Lowell built a big telescope in Arizona, partly to look at Mars. He really thought the canals were dug by Martians.

Then came all the crazy books and movies about

Mars and Martians. Ever heard of a book called *War of the Worlds*? H. G. Welles wrote it in 1898. In 1947, the story was made into a radio drama that scared people half to death. People thought Martians were really invading!

Even as late as the 1960s, people wondered about Mars. Astronomers with powerful telescopes could see greenish stuff on the planet. Maybe it was plants?

Nope. Sorry. And the canals weren't dug by Martians, either. Scientists figured that out when the first Mars probes flew by the planet. These tiny spaceships weren't big enough for people, of course. But they did have good cameras.

The first six tries failed, both American and Russian. The first spaceship to make it was called *Mariner 4*. It took eight months to get there, but this probe took the first closeup snapshots of Mars. Pretty cool!

Next came *Mariner 6, 7*, and *8*, and then the first try at a landing: the Russian *Mars 2* lander, in 1971. But *ka-pow! Mars 2*'s braking rockets didn't work. The lander was the first man-made Mars wreck.

The *Mars 3* lander a month later did better. It landed okay, and it managed to send back twenty seconds of video before it quit. Better than nothing. And better than *Mars 4, 6*, and 7. *Mars 4* missed the planet.

Mars 6 failed on the way down. *Mars 7* missed, too.

Get the picture yet? This is tricky stuff!

But try, try again. The American *Viking 2* landed fine in 1975 and sent home plenty of nifty photos. And after a few more goofs, we really got it right with the Mars *Pathfinder* mission in 1996. That's when the U.S. landed a six-wheeled buggy named the *Sojourner*, which wheeled around the surface for four months.

But be careful. A later mission, the *Mars Climate Orbiter*, crashed into Mars in September 1999. How? The people on Earth steering the *Orbiter* mixed up feet and meters, or miles and kilometers. Whoops!

There's more to come, though. In fact, a Mars spaceship is probably on its way to the planet as you read this. And NASA really wants to figure out how to land *people* on Mars!

If so, they probably won't find any Martian cities. No Martian footprints, either. But signs of life? Could be. Little green mossy things? Some ice chunks? Maybe.

Still, no matter where we go in space, no matter what scientists think they're looking for, you know what we'll always end up finding?

God's "fingerprints" on everything. After all, He made it.

Even Mars.

Want to find out more about Mars and space? Then check out:

- Send Your Name to Mars (on the Web at *www.spacekids.hq.nasa.gov/2001*). Tells how to get your name on a CD that's really going to Mars!
- Johnson Space Center (on the Web at *www.jsc.nasa.gov/pao/students*). Cool kids' links to everything from shuttle info to the latest on the *International Space Station.*

And the Coded Message Is . . .

You think this ASTROKIDS adventure is over? Not a chance. Uh-uh! No way. Negative. Nope. Because here's the plan: We'll give you the directions, you find the words. Write them all on a piece of paper. They form a secret message that has to do with *The Zero-G Headache*. If you think you got it right, log on to *www.coolreading.com* and follow the instructions there. You'll receive free ASTROKIDS wallpaper for your computer and a sneak peek at the next ASTROKIDS adventure. It's that simple!

WORD 1:
chapter 3, paragraph 1, word 2 ____________

WORD 2:
chapter 10, paragraph 29, word 1 ____________

WORD 3:
chapter 4, paragraph 2, word 39 ____________

WORD 4:
chapter 1, paragraph 14, word 13 ____________

WORD 5:
chapter 12, paragraph 6, word 27 ____________

WORD 6:
chapter 5, paragraph 49, word 10 ____________

WRITE IT ALL HERE:

____

____

(Hint: Tag says to look it up in *5:21 roc 1*. It's in the *elbib*.)

Contact Us!

If you have questions for the author or just want to say hi, feel free to contact him at Bethany House Publishers, 11400 Hampshire Avenue South, Minneapolis, MN 55438, United States of America, EARTH. Please include a stamped, self-addressed envelope if you'd like a reply. Or log on to Robert's intergalactic Web site at *www.coolreading.com*.

Launch Countdown

AstroKids 3: *The Wired Wonder Woof*

When a Galaxian trader-pirate visits *CLEO-7* in his mysterious spaceship, the AstroKids wonder why he is so interested in their new dog, Zero-G.

Sure, the cute little canine is smart—make that *very* smart. Especially since he can talk, thanks to his cool voice box. But the AstroKids agree: Zero-G is not for sale.

Or is he? Mir, the station commander's son, is not so sure. The smooth-talking space pirate doesn't seem so bad, really. And he offers to give Mir an amazing gift—all Mir has to do is get him the puppy.

But when Mir takes the eyeball cam for a secret spin aboard the Galaxian's ship, he realized he's made a terrible mistake.

Is it too late to save the wired wonder woof?

Series for Young Readers*
From Bethany House Publishers

THE ADVENTURES OF CALLIE ANN
by Shannon Mason Leppard

Readers will giggle their way through the true-to-life escapades of Callie Ann Davies and her many North Carolina friends.

ASTROKIDS™
by Robert Elmer

Space scooters? Floating robots? Jupiter ice cream? Blast into the future for out-of-this-world, zero-gravity fun with the AstroKids on space station *CLEO-7*.

BACKPACK MYSTERIES
by Mary Carpenter Reid

This excitement-filled mystery series follows the mishaps and adventures of Steff and Paulie Larson as they strive to help often-eccentric relatives crack their toughest cases.

THE CUL-DE-SAC KIDS
by Beverly Lewis

Each story in this lighthearted series features the hilarious antics and predicaments of nine endearing boys and girls who live on Blossom Hill Lane.

JANETTE OKE'S ANIMAL FRIENDS
by Janette Oke

Endearing creatures from the farm, forest, and zoo discover their place in God's world through various struggles, mishaps, and adventures.

RUBY SLIPPERS SCHOOL
by Stacy Towle Morgan

Join the fun as home-schoolers Hope and Annie Brown visit fascinating countries and meet inspiring Christians from around the world!

THREE COUSINS DETECTIVE CLUB®
by Elspeth Campbell Murphy

Famous detective cousins Timothy, Titus, and Sarah-Jane learn compelling Scripture-based truths while finding—and solving—intriguing mysteries.

*(ages 7–10)

Series for Middle Graders* From BHP

Adventures Down Under • by Robert Elmer
When Patrick McWaid's father is unjustly sent to Australia as a prisoner in 1867, the rest of the family follows, uncovering action-packed mystery along the way.

Adventures of the Northwoods • by Lois Walfrid Johnson
Kate O'Connell and her stepbrother Anders encounter mystery and adventure in northwest Wisconsin near the turn of the century.

An American Adventure Series • by Lee Roddy
Hildy Corrigan and her family must overcome danger and hardship during the Great Depression as they search for a "forever home."

Bloodhounds, Inc. • by Bill Myers
Hilarious, hair-raising suspense follows brother-and-sister detectives Sean and Melissa Hunter in these madcap mysteries with a message.

Girls Only! • by Beverly Lewis
Four talented young athletes become fast friends as together they pursue their Olympic dreams.

Mandie Books • by Lois Gladys Leppard
With over five million sold, the turn-of-the-century adventures of Mandie and her many friends will keep readers eager for more.

Promise of Zion • by Robert Elmer
Following WWII, thirteen-year-old Dov Zalinsky leaves for Palestine—the one place he may still find his parents—and meets the adventurous Emily Parkinson. Together they experience the dangers of life in the Holy Land.

The Riverboat Adventures • by Lois Walfrid Johnson
Libby Norstad and her friend Caleb face the challenges and risks of working with the Underground Railroad during the mid–1800s.

Trailblazer Books • by Dave and Neta Jackson
Follow the exciting lives of real-life Christian heroes through the eyes of child characters as they share their faith with others around the world.

The Twelve Candles Club • by Elaine L. Schulte
When four twelve-year-old girls set up a business of odd jobs and babysitting, they uncover wacky adventures and hilarious surprises.

The Young Underground • by Robert Elmer
Peter and Elise Andersen's plots to protect their friends and themselves from Nazi soldiers in World War II Denmark guarantee fast-paced action and suspenseful reads.

*(ages 8–13)